Rita Francis Mosscockle

The Golden Quest

And other Poems

Rita Francis Mosscockle

The Golden Quest
And other Poems

ISBN/EAN: 9783337401412

Printed in Europe, USA, Canada, Australia, Japan

Cover: Foto ©Andreas Hilbeck / pixelio.de

More available books at **www.hansebooks.com**

THE GOLDEN QUEST

AND OTHER POEMS

And the angel that was sent unto me, whose name was Uriel, gave me an answer, and said, "Thy heart hath gone too far in this world, and thinkest thou to comprehend the way of the Most High?"

Then said I, "Yea, my Lord."

Then said he unto me, "Go thy way, weigh me the weight of the fire, or measure me the blast of the wind, or call me again the day that is past."—2 ESDRAS, chap. iv.

THE GOLDEN QUEST

AND OTHER POEMS

BY

MRS. MOSS-COCKLE

AUTHOR OF "FANTASIAS"

LONDON

KEGAN PAUL, TRENCH, TRÜBNER & CO., Ltᴅ.

1890

CONTENTS.

———•◦•———

THE GOLDEN QUEST.

I.

LET me stay awhile to wander through this tangled
maze of life,—
Here in peace, with God to guide me—far from all
the mundane strife.

II.

Thus to taste those magic waters from the pure
Pierian spring;
Till in quest of life's Elixir, Heav'n its golden fruit
shall fling.

III.

Or on Mount Parnassus lying, listen to the bells
sublime,
Pealing down its lofty steeple, truths that echo through
all time.

IV.

With the wide world's wild pulsation, throbbing
    through the mortal years,
Light shall gild the far horizon, radiating sorrow's
    tears.

V.

As the wind blows where it listeth, who can say, lo
    here — or there ?
So the mighty spirit rushes, none can track him to his
    lair.

VI.

Life is short and time is speeding, lightly brushing
    down the hours,—
Till the trees stand stark and leafless, crownless and
    despoil'd, the bow'rs.

VII.

Memory stays but pleasures vanish, slowly, surely, one
    by one ;
And the progress of the nations, darts aloft from sun
    to sun.

VIII.

Eyes of Lynceus or Argus, give me that I penetrate
Through the wonderland of knowledge—thus my soul
    to elevate.

IX.

What is life, a dream? A platform whereon each
    must play a part ;
Holding self behind an ægis, off to ward the foeman's
    dart.

X.

Shuffling vainly for the trump card, in the fev'rish
    game of gain ;
Losing all that is most worthy, in the ignominious
    strain.

XI.

Daily nursing carking sorrow nestling in the buds of
    joy ;
Not a flower without a canker—nought of bliss without
    alloy.

XII.

Breathless haste, the great crowd hustling one another
    down the tide ;
Till some oasis they pant for, lying smiling at their
    side.

XIII.

Some soft pause for thinking—praying—some sweet
    lull of laden life ;
In the longing and pursuing, in the struggling and
    the strife.

XIV.

Here, a handshake, a smile, a word ; there, a frown,
    a shrug, a sigh ;
Here, the ring of a rippling laugh ; there, a moan and
    wailing cry.

XV.

Life and light for a little while—vapour merely, or a
    breath ;
Pulsing veins in the morning prime—and at night,
    the hush of death.

XVI.

Hard, frozen hearts beating around, tunèd to an ice-
bound world ;
Would they care if you died of cold, or in Lethe forth
were hurl'd ?

XVII.

Stoop and aid you to rise, would they, or e'en soil
their dainty hands?
They would rather bind you the more, manacled with
iron bands.

XVIII.

Abjectly ill full many lie on the wide highway of
life ;
But Society turns her head—and the misery grows
more rife.

XIX.

Ah, kind hearts, true hearts are few; never till their
light is gone,
Do we perceive the aureole that around their fore-
heads shone.

XX.

As a flow'r 'tis true we come; we bud,—we blossom—
    and we die;
But the falling seed will spring, a plant immortal in
    the sky.

XXI.

That we shall return I hold it, bearing forth the
    sheaves we've sown,—
Wheat and tares in that great Harvest when the Lord
    makes up His own.

XXII.

Of agnostics, what an army! crawling on the beaten
    sod;
With their finite knowledge seeking for the hidden
    truth of God.

XXIII.

Do they deem that nothing liveth that their narrow
    minds can't site?
How can finite understanding think to grasp the
    Infinite?

XXIV.

Storming with their paltry pellets, truth that meets
  them undismay'd ;
Futile fight against the Highest, better leave it
  unessay'd.

XXV.

Truth is proven by a witness which hies not from east
  or west ;
Not here—or there—but a spirit born of God, within
  the breast.

XXVI.

What a swarm of flashing fireflies singe their wings in
  rays that are,—
But the flicker of a rushlight which to them shines
  forth a star.

XXVII.

Shall we then dissect the lily, thinking limb from
  limb to tear,—
That the plan of all creation may unveil its secret
  there

XXVIII.

On a system which our groping, grovelling minds can
  never gauge;
God unfolds from one the other,—as He opens age
  from age.

XXIX.

But that man from brute evolvèd, can a sapient light
  affirm ;
Think you souls come forth of any but of Him from
  whom they germ ?

XXX.

On the summit of a mountain, lo I stand and view
  below,—
All the people flit as insects, restless, ceaseless to and
  fro.

XXXI.

Castles loom as puny ant-hills, trains and carriages
  as toys,—
In a state of constant motion, as propell'd by little
  boys.

XXXII.

And one thought that presses on me, seems to
conjure life to view
From a diff'rent standpoint, lending God's own mirror
clear and true.

XXXIII.

How infinitesimal are we! what minutiæ in His
Hand
Who took from dust to form of dust, His own Image
on the land.

XXXIV.

Out from protoplasm growing, peers the blade and
then the car;.
Slow unfolding—slow expanding—till develop'd form
appear.

XXXV.

From the lesser to the greater, evermore the ages
roll
In perpetual evolution, deep'ning, broad'ning out the
whole.

XXXVI.

All things perish in the using, moulded as we are of
    clay;
Only spirit actuating all our doings, lives alway.

XXXVII.

Mind doth never touch the body, toucheth not at any
    point;
Yet the motive power supplieth, fills with oil the
    empty joint.

XXXVIII.

O ye men of science probing deep within those
    wounds sublime;
When shall carping bring solution to the problems
    deep of time?

XXXIX.

Say, shall Darwin over Paley, triumph in his learned
    code?
Both may point to us diversely, up to God, the self-
    same road.

XL.

And if species now existing, did from forms primordial
    rise ;
God breathed breath into their nostrils and shot sight
    into their eyes.

XLI.

Reason out a fourth dimension in the wilderness of
    space ;
Argue from a syllogism, all hypotheses of race.

XLII.

Is it worth a lifetime's study, but to find when life
    is o'er,
We are little more than children digging on a bound-
    less shore ?

XLIII.

What though sceptics rave with wisdom, better be a
    child to glow
With the happiness of Heaven, than their heresies to
    know.

XLIV.

O faint and feeble little men, 'neath those vivid
    spheres on high,
'Twere well to humbly then confess, " Lord, how poor
    a thing am I."

XLV.

What are we but infants crying on the mother lap of
    earth ;
Infants in life, infants in death, infants as we were
    at birth ?

XLVI.

Mighty chain connecting all things—motive power of
    good and ill ;
Man is crown'd with God-like glory of the majesty
    of Will.

XLVII.

Descartes maintain'd free-will to be th' image true of
    Deity ;
Tree of life whose magic fruit is death and immor-
    tality.

XLVIII.

On the pole the ego reareth, doth our fate for ever
   turn ;
We, the outcome of the ages, strike the sparks that
   deathless burn.

XLIX.

If Will were not, and we were but puppets dancing
   on a board,—
Then no responsibility—punishment—nor yet reward.

L.

Truly are our acts our judges ; and our Nemesis we
   call—   .
From the deepest depths of darkness, or from Heav'n
   above us all.

LI.

Whence come cries and shrieks so piercing, that the
   air with wailing, smokes ?—
Crawling—curling round and up—till the fume sul-
   phuric chokes.

LII.

With sin and death the city heaves, paved with tear-
    drops are its ways;
And o'er the shining surface rolls a weary world its
    weary days.

LIII.

The little children cry for food, stones you give them
    —and not bread;
Breaking are their tender hearts, but their misery's on
    your head.

LIV.

Give them air, the stifled children—gasping in their
    stenching sty;
Give them space to play as blithely as the happy
    birds on high.

LV.

Sad are tears on aged faces; how far sadder on the
    young,—
Little lives that find too cruel, earth's rude mantle
    round them flung.

LVI.

" Feed my lambs," the Saviour said; but to drain the
   glass of pleasure,
You disburse all coin you have—and thus perish in
   the measure.

LVII.

In a whirlpool thousands languish, see the waters
   suck them up;
They are smiling as they drink it—the sweet poison
   in the cup.

LVIII.

They are dancing on the summit of the chasm as they
   go;
See, they near it—they turn reeling—and they dis-
   appear below !

LIX.

How the sun shines on the surface that secretes the
   victims well;
While a dirge-like singing mingles with the ocean's
   funeral knell.

LX.

And the air with sighs is laden, as the dark waves
 splash at night,—
Spirits passing and repassing, leave their phantom
 trail of light.

LXI.

Hark, the sound of rebel voices clamouring for a
 gilded goal ;
They a tinsel crown desiring, thus would barter e'en
 their soul.

LXII.

Mammon is the god they worship, bowing to the calf
 of gold,—
With the same profane obeisance as the Jews in days
 of old.

LXIII.

Canker-worms that gnaw and nibble, eating up our
 very life ;
Money-grubs are you that eat us—money-suckers
 germing strife.

LXIV.

Note obsequious attentions, blandest smiles so fair
    unfold ;
One eye suing for your favour, while the other 's on
    your gold.

LXV.

Lucre wears the garb of friendship—poor ass in a
    lion's skin ;
But the ears obtrude too rudely from the shoddy
    mane within.

LXVI.

Off, ye swarm of flies thus feeding on the meat your
    mouths corrode ;
Money is for good intended, not to lie a stagnant
    load.

LXVII.

Clothe the naked, feed the hungry, shelter those who
    are opprest ;
With your gold let best works flourish, and God's love
    will add the rest.

LXVIII.

Seek not far for some to succour, they are crying at
our gate;
They are dying on our threshold — while we know not
half their state.

LXIX.

Sinking souls and starving bodies—reeking misery
and woe;
God is asking through His children, for the love you
will not show.

LXX.

Coarsest raiment oft disguises those whom He has
pleased to dress
With the beauty-hue of Heaven—saintly robes of
righteousness.

LXXI.

Fill'd with pain untold and rending, is the pulsing
world around;
All its want and anguish reading us a lesson most
profound.

LXXII.

That we lose no chance of aiding, smoothing with
    our little best,—
Any pillow hard and thorny, any couch of sad unrest.

LXXIII.

Give us friendship—hearts as sterling, burning with
    unflick'ring ray;
Loyal in all thought and action, true to-morrow as
    to-day.

LXXIV.

With electric current rises kindred soul that answers
    mine;
Eye meets eye, and searching deeply, peerless trea-
    sures I divine.

LXXV.

Converse sweet on subjects closely lying near the
    hearts of each;
Much to hear and learn and ponder; much to tell,
    and much to teach.

LXXVI.

May not friendship be Platonic, as the Dorians' mode
  that fired
Plato's perfect letters teeming with romantic love
  inspired?

LXXVII.

Love that holds us with its passion, in the sunshine
  of to-day,
Will it flourish in the gloaming when life spends her
  golden ray?

LXXVIII.

Will it grasp the trembling fingers, smooth the silver-
  banded brow?
Flower of flowers that softly shaketh glitt'ring dews
  of love-drops now.

LXXIX.

Such a gift—the fairest, rarest, Heav'n-born bloom of
  love on earth;
Making e'en the beggar maiden worthy of Cophetua's
  birth.

LXXX.

Love, a lion in your strength, a lamb by silken ribbon
    led;
An angel of the inner self, has your finer senses wed.

LXXXI.

Hear the weary, weary beating of the maiden's gentle
    heart;
Fie upon the cruel wooer who has aim'd the poison'd
    dart.

LXXXII.

She will still the wild pulsation, press her hand upon
    her brow;
But the light of her existence will have vanish'd from
    her now.

LXXXIII.

She will seize a noble mission, with an earnest loving
    zeal;
Crushing down her heart's fair blossoms, in the work
    for others' weal.

LXXXIV.

Woman stakes her all, her treasure, on one altar here
  below ;
Loving once, she loves for ever with a radiating
  glow.

LXXXV.

Ah my darling, how you won me—won me from my
  proud estate ;
Till my will was merged in tracing out for you a
  happy fate.

LXXXVI.

And the cold heart melting in me, ran in rivers through
  my life ;
Love-lit currents rippling fondly, round my queen—
  my own true wife.

·LXXXVII.

Dante's Beatrice, Petrarch's Laura, worshipp'd as they
  were—afar,
Were but poets' dream-creations—shadow-forms to
  what you are.

LXXXVIII.

Something tangible, I hold you—angel and companion
    tried;
Wisest counsellor and helpmeet—truest friend and
    dearest guide.

LXXXIX.

Man is what a woman makes him, motive power of
    the machine
She who stands at helm directing, with stout heart
    and eye serene.

XC.

" Born to rule, but not for battle," Ruskin deems of
    woman's sphere ;
She should let this puissance crown her with a value
    doubly dear.

XCI.

Are the rights of women, truly, thrusting home the
    wrongs of men ?
Nay, 'tis only jealous carping that would shut them
    out again.

XCII.

Shut them out from boundless treasures with which
 wisdom's fields are white;
Shut them in to serve as Phyllis, rock the children,
 day and night.

XCIII.

Once the slaves of household tyrants, in their minis-
 tries opprest;
Deem'd incapable of rising to the level of his quest.

XCIV.

Now proved worthy of presiding at the councils of the
 state;
In the woman's crown of honour, gleams the jewel
 of the great.

XCV.

O my sisters, with your dowry—pow'r to do and stay
 so much;
Why should vice breathe in your presence, why should
 daily life be such?

XCVI.

Better far than protestations, grander than fine pre-
cepts giv'n,
Is the silent sweet example of a life that points to
Heav'n.

XCVII.

In each soul there dwells the hidden, closely-hugg'd,
—far out of sight ;
None of us unveil that treasure to the cold hard stare
of light.

XCVIII.

Two selves pulsing in one body; one, the spirit of
the earth ;
And the other that pure essence,—offshoot of immortal birth.

XCIX.

Raging fiercely in their prison, striving each one to
prevail ;
Sir Galahad no stronger strove to obtain the Holy
Grail.

C.

Stamp it down O gentle spirit, trample on the seed
  of sin ;
Make the spark divine to triumph, let the angel in
  us win.

CI.

Ah, there gnaws a growing craving, buried deeply in
  the breast;
'Tis the burden of a burning to express the unex-
  press'd.

CII.

Flash our words athwart the silence of th' luminous,
  mighty world ;
Wing'd with flame their fiery arrows, and their purple
  crest unfurl'd.

CIII.

Swiftly speeds their bubbling current coursing through
  our throbbing veins;
Shiv'ring many a hope to atoms with the clanking of
  their chains.

CIV.

The seed they sow, the tares they sow, whither fly,
    we cannot say ;
But the scatter'd grain we know will swell the harvest
    store one day.

CV.

The world is revolutionized ! once blue blood held
    sovereign sway ;
But now alas, vox populi cries that " we're as good as
    they."

CVI.

Would He who modell'd from the first, clay wrought
    of diff'rent classes ;
Approve of tables He set up, overturnèd by the
    masses ?

CVII.

The busy mart of life is block'd with a seething,
    surging sea ;
And the world's great burden is the suff'ring of
    humanity.

CVIII.

One long cry that rises ever, swelling volumes in its
    tone,—

Pierces through the darkness, falling stunn'd with light
    before the Throne.

CIX.

Ceaseless struggling, striving, stumbling, in the race
    before us here ;

Maddest stampede ! tramping over human lives in our
    career.

CX.

Who can say in the millennium, if Utopian codes
    will reign ;

And if truth and right unshackled, will shine out
    star-lit again ?

CXI.

A perfect hierarchy it seems, far in my vision rises ;—

When no hydra-beasts will stalk, raving fiends in
    saints' disguises.

CXII.

When the truth undimm'd, unerring, shall uphold her
 glass to time ;
Lamb and Lion correlating—stretch'd before one
 hearth sublime.

CXIII.

When happiness will be unmark'd by pale sorrow's
 tearful stain ;
And love will drink nepenthe draughts, with its own
 true love again.

CXIV.

What is happiness, we ask—the summum bonum all
 would seek ; .
Dwells it in the stately castle, or in cottage of the
 meek ?

CXV.

Is it wrapt in rank or jewels, downy couch or dainty
 fare ?
You may seek in these to find it—but know well, it is
 not there.

CXVI.

Aristotle deems it reigneth, over all things proudly
tow'rs,

In exerting all the noblest, all the highest of our
pow'rs.

CXVII.

But relegate it how you will—its true essence is,
defin'd,

Laid in the heart that stay'd on God, there holds
perfect peace enshrined.

CXVIII.

Ah vain hopes and aspirations! what avails if faith
is fled?

Crowns and kings and thrones must mingle with
the ashes of the dead.

CXIX.

All things flow in one strong current which no mortal
can arrest,

To the touchstone of all knowledge—to the sepulchre
of rest.

CXX.

Who will call us false accusers of an age whose evil
  aim,
Is to drag through dust God's glory, and with zeal His
  Word defame?

CXXI.

Trampling down with wanton fury, pearls more
  precious far than life;
Hurling paltry preachments—pand'ring to the wild
  desire for strife.

CXXII.

Strife, I say! what strive with angels? Principalities
  and pow'rs, .
Are but hollow-sounding cymbals, blasted rocks and
  tumbling tow'rs.

CXXIII.

Parley with the saints of Heaven—derogate the truths
  they taught;
Interlard, transmute at pleasure, till God's Word is
  sin-inwrought?

CXXIV.

Casting weaklings low in darkness; laughing at
 their blank despair;
Seeds Saturnine sowing broadcast—till rank poison
 fumes the air.

CXXV.

What more vile, save for the tenet that the Christ was
 only man?
Mad seducers of salvation, smear His robe you never
 can.

CXXVI.

You would hypnotize our spirit, with your foul and
 wicked spells,
(If you could) till we admitted all the lies your black
 art tells.

CXXVII.

Blind Socinians! could such marvels never seen or
 work'd before,
Emanate from any other than the God who broke
 death's door?

CXXVIII.

Would you suck our life-blood from us, dash the cup
    He quaff'd to give
Such redemption—such salvation, that all who believe,
    may live ?

CXXIX.

Anti-Christ is risen roaring like a lion through the
    land ;
But small David slew a giant, with a pebble in his
    hand.

CXXX.

And what matter that he roareth ? with an arrow
    wing'd with light,
We can pierce him, pin him helpless, till he howls
    in wild affright.

CXXXI.

Darkness, doubt, phantasmal horrors crowd the little
    night of time ;
But at morn the shadows fleeing, shall break forth
    the light sublime.

CXXXII.

Go not down in deepest dudgeon, O most mighty
    mother age ;
Weeping o'er the gruesome follies acted on a pinch-
    beck stage.

CXXXIII.

Life is fairer, stronger, truer, as the earth-veil slips
    away ;
Opening up a golden vision—palaces of endless day :

CXXXIV.

Deeper love and nobler longings, all unfelt in sunny
    spring
When the careless heart is leaping in a hall where
    death-knells ring.

CXXXV.

When the odour of the roses from the garden steep'd
    in light,
Flames the thirsty, thoughtless spirit, with a false
    but fond delight.

CXXXVI.

Pluck the flowers, O foolish children, and their beauty
    is laid low ;
Take the blossom in your fingers, and behold, the
    bloom must go.

CXXXVII.

Kill by slow degrees the carnal—sink the grosser
    in the great ;
Till the fleshly faints and falters in the full soul's
    fuller state.

CXXXVIII.

Bring me forth a wreath immortal, from the golden
    fields of light ;
* Let me place it on her forehead, as she sleeps there
    wrapp'd in white.

CXXXIX.

She shall lie though stilly—queenly, in a pompous,
    solemn state ;
While for her the cannon booming, shall roar out
    all honour great.

    * The Church, the bride of Christ.

CXL.

Such a smile—a smile of angels, I can see upon her
    face,
That no shade of care shall darken, and no sorrow
    shall efface.

CXLI.

On her breast the cross is gleaming, emblem of her
    living love ;
Of the battles and confusion—of the strife wherein
    she strove.

CXLII.

And the white rose softly nestling in the ringlet o'er
    her brow,
Is no purer than her spirit—infinitely perfect now.

CXLIII.

Stay a moment—on the shimmer of her faultless
    flowing dress,
Drops a stain of ruby colour—life-blood of her
    Righteousness.

CXLIV.

It has touch'd her—woke her—flamed her with un-
    utterable life !
See, she rises,—bathed in glory, snapping e'en death's
    flashing knife.

CXLV.

I have found it—life's Elixir—in the stain that stung
    her rest ;
O Eureka ! O Eureka ! it is here—the Golden Quest.

A HARVEST HYMN.

This Hymn is set to music as a March and Trio for organ and full chorus, by R. Graham Harvey. Published by Hart and Co.

(MARCH.)

LORD, with joy our thanks we offer,
    For the gifts which Thou dost strew;
Fruits, the golden fields are yielding,
    Ever year by year anew.

Hear us in Thy love confiding,
    As we view our garners bless'd;
Thou who sendest rain that bringest,
    Ears of corn in beauty dress'd.

(TRIO.)

Love, such rich wealth of fullest blessing falling
    On earth's fair fields and on the harvest store,—
Rings out the praise o'er all the wide world calling,
    Of that dear Hand which feeds us evermore.

Lord, on that day when the bright sheaves dividing,
    Rank tares from out the ripen'd wheat are riv'n ;
O may we be for aye with Thee abiding,
    The golden grain within the fields of Heav'n.

(March.)

Praise the Saviour—praise His goodness,
    Praise His name for evermore ;
For the seed-time and the harvest,
    For the sunshine and the shower.

A STAR REVERIE.

FROM my small window yesternight,
    I look'd out on the stars ;
The firmament shone clear and bright,
    Fleck'd by long golden bars.
      The sombre shadows leapt,
      Where the pale Dryads kept
A festival of fays, within the ilex-wood,
Till all the leaves were rustling as their mood.

The long paulonia blossoms slept,—
    Beneath the star-gemm'd sphere.
The od'rous breezes softly sang
    To my tired spirit here.
      "O light ! O star of life !"
      I cried—" and is there rife,
A tangible, a tawny tangled web to twine
Around my sighing soul, and make it all divine ? "

The moon went out in clouds, and up
  A dreary darkness rush'd—
Shrouding the world; and all my heart
  Cowed down, crestfallen—crush'd.
    Though dense and dull the night,
    At morn it shall be light.
Sorrow must die as the dark must die, and ringing
With pealing preludes of praise, earth's voice was
  singing.

" Change," is the universal law;
  No time or state stands still;
The mystery of progression,
  Life's secret records fill.
    We hold the treasures sent,
    As jewels only lent—
To stud life's pathway here; and then enthroned
  afar—
There burns on everlasting hills, the brightest star.

THE LOVE THAT NEVER DIES.

These lines were written for an interpolated song in the Cantata "John Gilpin," music by R. Graham Harvey. Published by Hart and Co.

O VERY dear in springtime,
  Is the laughing blue-eyed bride ;
But dearer is she after,
  As they walk life side by side.
They draw fresh draughts for loving,
  As they find heart-gems declare,
The roses of such gladness,
  Are a coronal for care.
    It is not love
      That with time flies,
    Love is the love
      That never dies.

Love only grows the greater
  In the rolling tide of years ;
Love only lives for ever,
  That hath fought time's many fears.
And like a rushing river
  Flowing onward to the sea,—
Love stronger, purer, truer,
  Glides into eternity.
    It is not love
      That with time flies,
    Love is the love
      That never dies.

THE WEB OF LIFE.

LIFE is a web, wherein we weave
    The vital threads that stitch our fate ;
For good or ill, we intertwine
    The warp and woof of our estate.
Each fibre pulsing through the years,
Evokes the smiles or wrings the tears.

Ah ! could we weave our life of joys,
    Of sweets and dainties delicate,
Such dear delights might cloy the tastes,—
    For which the piquant feast was set ;
And we should die of our desires,
Consumèd in ten thousand fires.

Nay, rather let us weave the good,
    The common good of all mankind ;
The right intent, the honest heart,
    The deeds that only can be kind.
Thus by a magic weft to climb
To all most noble and sublime.

MY WIFE.

O DEEP within those clear, calm eyes,
    A bright flame burns ;
They flash the happy light around,
    Where'er she turns :
They hold me in a magic weft,
    Till I am drawn,—
Into the glory of her love,
    As night clasps dawn ;
Sinking her darkness silently
    To morn's fair face,
Till earth and sky are rosy-lit,
    With her embrace.
I contemplate her as she stands,
    My perfect wife.
God said it was not good to live
    Alone this life.

He gave a woman—man's best self,
    To fill that sphere,—
Which is the holiest and
    Of all, most dear.
The first, the nearest place of love,
    The honoured wife.
Ah ! that she still might hold that name,
    In that far life—
Where Christ hath said, all, angels are,
    No marriage reigns ;
He knows it not, who such pure joys
    And bliss attains.
But it may be that she, my wife,
    Will be more there
Than here, to me.   There may be e'en
    A place more fair,
A name more dear, a higher state
    Of union—more,
Above, and greater still than wife.
So true, she is—so pure, so good,
    In her combine
All those fair qualities which are
    Well-nigh sublime.

A wife should ever be as she, —
 Head, heart, and mind
To him who holds the golden key,
 Her gems to find.
An angel-ministrant to point
 The Heav'nward way, —
Through earth's night-time of tear-stain'd hours,
 To cloudless day.

NAPOLEON'S CONVICTION.*

HE read it—the great world's hero;
    He read of the Perfect Man
Incarnate in the Son of God;
    And as his keen eye ran—
Through all those mystic pages touch'd
    With fire from Heav'n's own shrine;
He closed the book, then gravely said,
    "Look you, I, men divine;
But this same Christ of whom I read,
    He is no man—but God."

      * Anecdote related of Napoleon I.

RHYME OF THE BRIDE.

DEAREST, on this happy day,
Would you have me wipe away
All the tears I cannot stay?

Would you see me cold and still,
When my fount of life you fill,—
With your troth and sweetest will?

Such a day recalls the years
When my love was dew'd with fears,
Which I wipe out with these tears.

In the home where fair hours sped,
Fancy took it in her head
To bind me with a golden thread.

E

And this thread is woven through
With a ray that doth imbue
My most perfect love of you.

Now upon this marriage-day,
Ere the love-chant dies away,
And the people for us pray ;

While the holy light doth rest
On these heads which God hath blest ;
Let us plead for what is best :

Best for you and best for me,
In the new life that shall be,
Earth's most perfect symphony.

May no ills or joys of life,
May no bitter words of strife,
Drift apart this man and wife.

That our fireside's ruddy blaze,
Glowing in a mellow'd haze,
Mirror love's enchanted gaze.

Which shall crown our silver'd hair,
With an aureole so rare,
Angels e'en might deem it fair.

Angels e'en might pause to see,
Hovering o'er us ceaselessly ;
How this love such love can be.

Then awhile to parted be,
In death's river—you and me ;
Through the golden gates to see

Life's true life, and love's true love, —
Where our souls, rejoin'd, shall move
In eternal bonds—above.

HOPE ON.

Hope on whatever be thy lot,
    Do not despair.
Heav'n, thy path below is lighting,
    And God is there.
Sorrows cannot stay to chide us,
    Nor tears for long ;
Soon the sighs shall break in singing
    One long sweet song.
Hope on, for far away on angel-wings,
Hope brings glad tidings of immortal things.

Hope on dear heart, beyond there lies
    All we desire ;
But we must to gain that glory,
    Pass through the fire.

First the sowing, then the reaping ;
    Night, ere morn's ray ;
Sorrow only crowns with gladness
    The perfect day.
Hope on, for far away on angel-wings,
Hope brings glad tidings of immortal things.

THE BEE AND THE ROSE.

"I LOVE you much," said the bee to the rose ;
  "I love you much, my dear ;
And I would kiss your downy cheek,
  If I might draw more near.
If I might come more near, my dear,
    If I might come more near."

The rose look'd pleased, for she open'd her leaves ;
  The bee flew in with glee ;
He stole the sweets and stung her heart,
  Then away off was he.
"I cannot linger here, my dear,
    I cannot linger here."

"O such is life," said the rose through her tears ;
  "We give our sweets away,
And barter all at pleasure's cost,
  Which never can repay.
But we cannot linger here, I fear,
  We cannot linger here."

THE CHILDREN SLEPT.

These lines were written on the Forest Gate disaster; and the episode related of the little boy who went back into the burning building, to fetch his friend, is said to be true.

CALMLY, sweetly, the children slept;
Swiftly, surely, the red flames crept,—
Writhing, wriggling their demon heads,
Closer around those little beds.

The smiling faces wore a light
Of pleasure born that fatal night;
To some bright scene they then had been,
Perchance to change the dull routine

Of weary days and hours that past,
Each one the same as was the last.
Thus hail'd with childhood's own delight,
Was that gay fête on that sad night.

To bed they went with hearts more gay,
Than they had known for many a day;
And rosy dreams of fairer hours,
Danced blithely 'mongst their new-found flowers.

A piercing shriek;—and then a choir
Of anguish'd cries rose higher, higher,—
Till smoke and voices fire and heat,
Lash'd through the air in one wild beat !

The tongues of flame devoured their prey
With ghastly relish, as they lay—
Unconscious of the danger round,
That made their gentle sleep profound.

Never to wake to see the day
Break through the rift of clouds away;
Never to know either tears or pain,
Wearisome days or nights again.

Taken 'midst dreams of a sunny world,
To the perfect glory above unfurl'd;
Where immortal flow'rs pervade the land,
And star the hair of the happy band.

Sav'd from the flames, a small boy stood—
But what now drove the mantling blood
Forth from his cheek?   "Ah! where is Jack,
My chum, my friend?—I must go back

And fetch him out"—so swiftly tore
The noble boy, through death's dark door;
For both the children fell a prey
To that conflagration's sway.

Full many heroes lie unknown
Beneath life's coldly carven stone;
And hearts beat high with nobler aim,
Than earthly annals do proclaim.

Fair sleeping children! up in Heav'n,
The light of God to you is giv'n;
Of such the kingdom is, and blest
Are they who find such perfect rest.

THE FIDDLER'S DREAM.

This song is set to music by R. Graham Harvey. Published by Hart and Co.

HE came to his home in the morning hours,
From a scene of the bright and gay ;
Where his fiddle had thrill'd some aching hearts,
And charm'd all their cares away.
He looked around on the desolate room,
That a young wife had left so bare ;
Now alas, the only delight he own'd,
Was the fiddle he claspèd there.
As he gently, lovingly laid it by,
A glimmer of dawning fell,
And lighted it up with a golden ray,
This old friend that he loved so well.

On his lonely pillow he lay asleep,
   But to dream of his darling wife ;
Of the sunny days in young hope's sweet time,
   And the fair after married life.
And it seems that he sees her listening,—
   With love's light in her beaming eye,
To the speaking tones of his fiddle's voice,
   In the Heavenly choir on high.
The same sweet strain he is playing again,
   That his dear one so much did love ;—
In the angel-band, of the better land ;
   In the sorrowless courts above.

THE LOVER AND THE MAID.

On a fair and rosy morning
    In the springtime of the year,
Came a lover to a maiden,
    Whisper'd words into her ear ;
That called such a glow of gladness,
    And won such a sweet reply,
All the roses in the garden
    Thought for her he fain would die.
" Will you wait awhile, my darling,
    Though my heart for you be sore,
Then to be for always with me,
    Nearest, dearest, evermore ? "

And she waited long and sadly,
    Waited years for his return ;
With his ring upon her finger,
    While her heart for him did burn.

But he came not, and she faded
  As a white rose bows her head ;
All the glory of her beauty,
  All her petals slowly shed.
What is all the good of loving,
  If love only lives a day ?
Men may lose their hearts then. find them ;
  But a woman loves alway.

THE DEATH OF LOVE.

SHALL we die if love is fled,
Sadly bow the weary head;
Think the world so cold and dark,
Without Cupid's lambent spark ?
Ah no.

Life is life when love is not;
And it holds some vernal spot,
Where forgetfulness shall twine
Fairest flowers upon her shrine.
O yes.

Love, a flimsy gleaming thing;
Ever darting on the wing,
Here and there—above, below;
Where it rests, we cannot know.
Ah no.

Angels' visits are as rare
As the love that true can bear
Time and change, and sorrow's tear
Strolling down a cheek once dear.
O yes.

Hold it fast when love is true.;
Happy if he comes to you ;
Many know him, few can say
That he lives beyond a day.
Ah no.

Die not then when love is fled ;
Dry the eyes and raise the head ;
Life is life when love is not,
And it holds some vernal spot.
O yes.

VITA BREVIS.

We come, we play our part, we smile, we weep,
we die;
Then 'neath the sod the mourners leave us there
to lie.

They heap the turf above, around the weary head;
While mournfully they say, "the soul to God is
fled."

They wear a woe-worn face to match their sombre
dress;
Till Time, the world's wound-healer makes the
sorrow less.

O such is life! like children building tow'rs of
sand,
The first great death-wave swoops us down from out
the land.

F

Onward flows all life towards the one ideal,—
Which doth substitute the seeming for the real.

The child before the man—the bud—and then the
    flow'r;
Mortal then immortal—death ere life evermore.

A BALLAD OF POETS.

GREAT soul—great beacon light that flames
The arching firmament of power—
That pales with its superior glow,
The lesser luminaries quite ;
Immortal Shakespeare, do I see
You pass in all your kingly state :
While treading closely on your heels,—
Comes Goethe with the princely mien,
The weird sparks playing on his brow ;
Bearing the scroll of his own " Faust."
And then, hand clasp'd in hand, there pass,—
Milton and Dante clothed with fire
That flashes light from Heav'n's own shrine, —
Until it burns in livid tongues,
Upon the hearth-stone of the world.
Then Shelley with his lyre that woke
The silence of the hills—and charm'd

As Orpheus, the very brutes,—
Passes in slow procession forth ;
With Tennyson the laurel-crown'd ;
And Byron bard of love, whose lays
Vibrate through all youth's golden days.
Heartbroken Keats, and bland Tom Moore,
Whose simple strains still draw a tear ;
With ploughman Burns who fann'd the spark
Ethereal, beneath his blouse.
Wordsworth—Longfellow—Whittier ;
Together with a glorious throng,
So dazzling—that my eyes I shade,
Before th' effulgence of their rays.
Thus higher do they grandly rise,
In one long shining company.
Above the grade of common things—
Above the earth—above the stars,
They bear in crucible divine,—
Their splendid incense, straight to God.

THE HOLY GARDEN OF SLEEP.

THERE 's rest in the tombs of the silent dead,
Where the willow waves her arms o'er their head ;
And the fairest flowers are strewn to prove,—
That death can never annihilate love.

A peace profound—yet so solemn and deep,
Reigns over this holy garden of sleep ;
That the tears of the living may not mate
To the sorrows and cares of mortal state.

As the white flow'rs droop on the lowly graves,
And the fresh rain all the green grass blades laves,—
So lying there dust to dust, they shall bring
From the buried seeds, fair blooms in the spring :

The spring immortal—the spring that will shine
For ever and ever on hills divine ;
When the poor weak bodies that we have sown,
Shall glorified rise—though the same—their own.

Thus rest in the holy garden, belov'd,—
Till the stigma of death be all remov'd ;
When the light that breaks on eternal day,
Shall chase the shadows of earth away.

LYRA ANGELICA.

THERE is a clash of music on the hills,
That vibrates softly, and the fresh air fills
With such a melody of many lyres,—
It thrills through all the soul's divine desires ;
Infusing such new life—such ecstasy,
I catch the tones of Heav'n's own minstrelsy.

The path below is sown with scarlet flow'rs
That twine their tendrils round the vernal bow'rs ;
Behind the blooms, the serpent-eyes gleam bright,—
But from above streams down the golden light
That withers them within their sockets,—so,
The way winds upward, and that way I go.

Some tears must fall—some breath must bow the trees ;
The sun disperses them ; then on the breeze
The night-wind sighs, and bursting through the dawn,—
Aurora bounds—and lo ! behold 'tis morn.

The gate is open of those mansions fair ;
Yet should I enter—dare I venture there,—

But for the King, my King who standing smiles
Without the portals, and my fear beguiles?
'Tis He, 'tis He, the wind may come and go ;
'Tis He, come gladness or come woe ;
Be long or short the way—or hard the sod,
What matter? since He is my King—my God.

THE END.

PRINTED BY WILLIAM CLOWES AND SONS, LIMITED,
LONDON AND BECCLES.

BY THE SAME AUTHOR.

———◆———

FANTASIAS.

Small crown 8vo. 2s. 6d.

This small volume of poems shows a cultivated and comprehensive taste, as the subjects of the verses include religion, classic mythology, and domestic incident. The poem placed first in the book is entitled " Follow Me," and includes a few dramatic representations of the response made by different ages and conditions in human life.—*The Queen.*

I have by the way, come across a charming little book : " Fantasias," by Mrs. Moss-Cockle, published very neatly by Kegan Paul, Trench, and Co., and full of gems which the mind may lay up and garner, and the soul be all the better of knowing, and the lips of repeating, and the heart of treasuring. It is a sweet and pure book—one such as is seldom met with in this age of lurid colouring, and sultry sentiment, and dangerous, insidious teaching : a book such as we should like our children to possess, and feel a safety and pleasure in the knowledge that they are occupied in studying. In my busy life, I have rarely time to read ; an occupied journalist is supposed to write *always* —without time to think, or read, or eat, or sleep, or even to pray—and he does it—is obliged to do it—and it is only when he occasionally takes up and tastes such sweet waters as these of which I am writing, that he knows and realises the unhealthiness of the Marah in which his tired faculties are so often steeped. To our readers, one and all, I say, get the book, and

turn down a leaf at " The Little Street-sweeper," " Aqua Vitæ,"
" The Child's Letter," " Trifles make the Sum of Life," and
" Mattie in the Cloisters." They are all good, and all beautiful.
—*Lady's Pictorial.*

In the small volume of poems christened " Fantasias," from
the pen of Mrs. Moss-Cockle, the opening verses " Follow Me,"
are the best. A good deal of deep, religious, and tender sentiment finds expression, and occasionally not without the ring of
genuine poetic feeling. But the lyrics are unequal, anon the
metre limps, here and there the idea is commonplace, and
sometimes the moral doubtful. The poet, for example, must
not kindle our sympathy for " The Little Street-sweeper," as if
the undiscriminating distribution of pence were a sacred duty.
Real charity is by no means so easy, and unfortunately perhaps,
it seldom lends itself to poetry.—*The Daily Telegraph.*

Some of the tender and pathetic verses contained in the little
volume entitled " Fantasias," are already familiar in the guise
of favourite songs, and it would be easy to point out in it many
others admirably adapted to be " wedded to sweet music," and
secure similar success to that attained by " The Days of Long
Ago," and " Changeless Still." That the author is capable of
more sustained effort and dramatic construction than can be
manifested in these short productions is proved by the first poem
of this book, " Follow Me," though a less ambitious choice of
subject would probably have given a more satisfactory result.
" A Dream of Apollo " furnishes perhaps the most poetically
conceived and carefully written specimen of Mrs. Moss-Cockle's
powers, whilst it must be admitted that the halting lines and
very imperfect rhythm of one or two effusions render their pub-
lication matter of regret. These instances, are however, by no
means of sufficiently frequent occurrence to mar the merit of the
whole work, or to prevent its recommendation to the numerous
class of readers who delight in simple and unpretentious versifi-
cation imbued with a tone of melancholy.—*Morning Post.*

3

The title is a very apt one, for the poems are full of strange fancies, many of them beautifully expressed. An age which is strongly marked by a love of materialism, with a strong spice of cynicism, is not likely to be favourable to poetry ; but the writer is a true poet. Many of the poems are marked by the highest Christian spirit.—*Western Morning News.*

The beautiful little poems contained in this small volume, are well worthy of notice. Each one has its own peculiar charm for a poetic mind, but a peculiar pathos is attached to one called " The Child's Letter."—*Court Journal.*